Uirapurú

Uirapurú

By P.K. Page

Illustrated by Kristi Bridgeman

oolichan
books

Let me tell you about a
beautiful bird,
an everlasting bird
that lives deep in
the rain forests
of Brazil.

Those who have heard it sing call it 'Uirapurú' because that is the sound of its song:

"Oor a poor oo" "Oora poor ooooo."

There were some who thought it sang, 'You're a poor you.' Others thought it sang, 'You're a pure you.' Still others thought that it was just singing.

Many people went in search of it. Some never
returned. Those who did, told of its beautiful
song sung in the black of the night—a song they
would never forget.

'Oora poor oooo.'

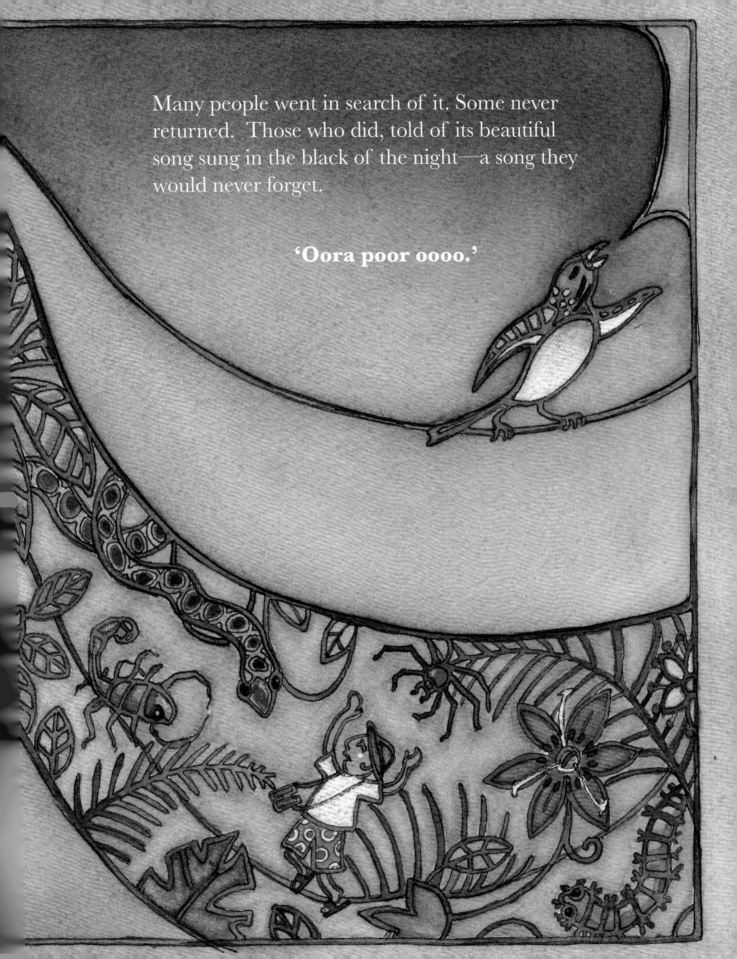

One day a group of boys decided to catch the bird. They had nets and bows and arrows and they wanted the bird alive or dead.

For many days and many nights they traveled into the rain forest. Then one night they heard a sound so sweet they thought it could only be the song of the Uirapurú. They drew closer and closer to the source of the music but instead of a bird they saw an old, old man sitting at the foot of a tree and playing a flute.

"What are you doing?" the boys asked.

"I am trying to play the song of the Uirapurú," the old man said.

"If you play the notes, will the bird come?" the boys asked, for they could see that in this way the old man might help them.

"Sadly, no," the old man said. "For I would have to play the song perfectly and that I cannot do. The Uirapurú will come only for another Uirapurú and it is said that there is only one left in all the world. And if his song dies, the world, as we know it, will end. So I listen and listen and try to copy it exactly."

The boys were angry with the old man and drove him
away. But they were excited by the idea that there was
only one Uirapurú in all the world and they were even
more eager to catch it.

The forest seemed quiet and lonely with the old man gone and very dark indeed and soon the boys fell asleep—half-listening, even as they slept, for the song of the Uirapurú.

What wakened them instead were astonishing sounds—clicks and buzzes and squeaks and hoots.

And when they opened their eyes
the full moon shone on an even more
astonishing sight— a young woman—
as shining and white as the moon itself,
and around her, flying and flapping
and hopping and running
were all the creatures of the night.
There were shiny black beetles
  and large pale moths
    and tiny green tree frogs
    and velvet moles
      and spotted nightjars
        and owls so small you could
          hold them in your hand.

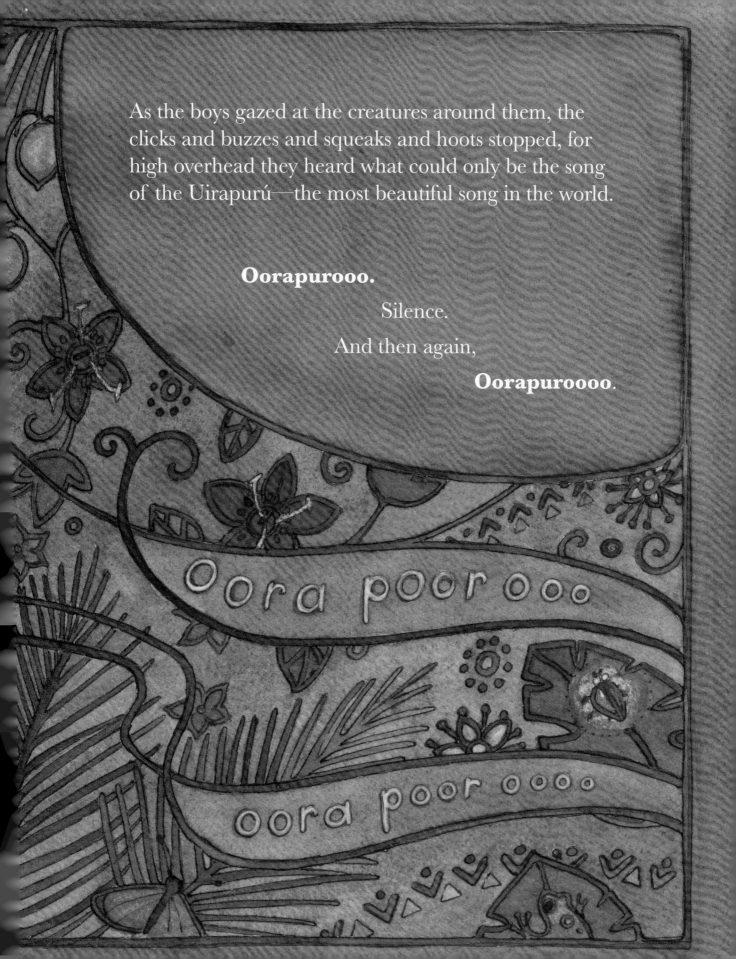

As the boys gazed at the creatures around them, the clicks and buzzes and squeaks and hoots stopped, for high overhead they heard what could only be the song of the Uirapurú—the most beautiful song in the world.

Oorapurooo.

Silence.

And then again,

Oorapuroooo.

Oora poor ooo

oora poor oooo

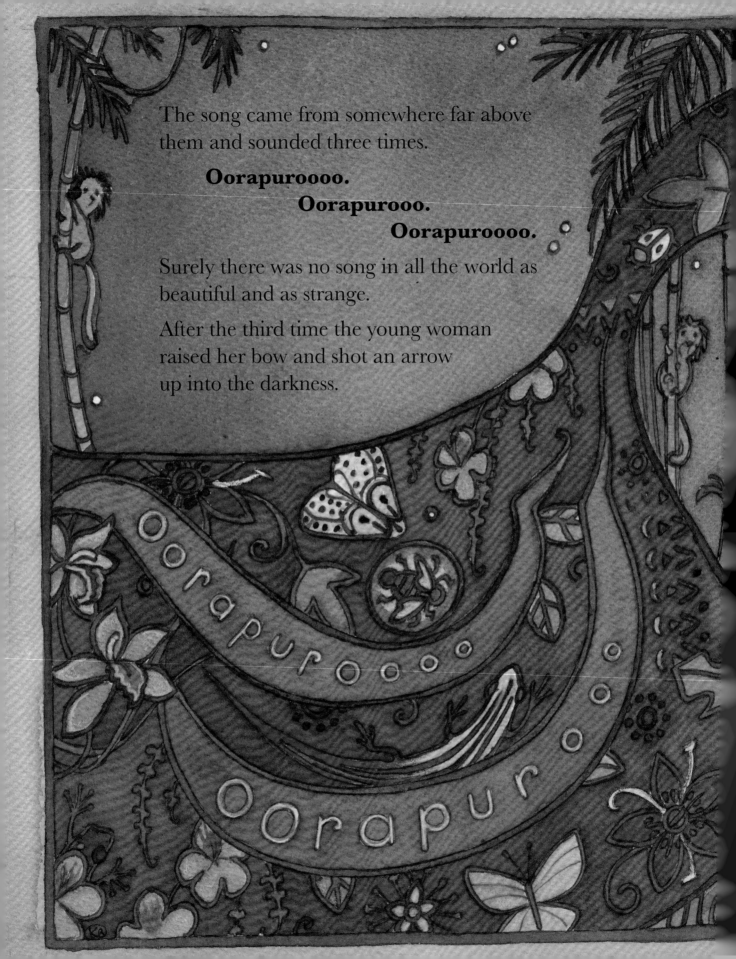

The song came from somewhere far above
them and sounded three times.

Oorapuroooo.

        Oorapurooo.

                Oorapuroooo.

Surely there was no song in all the world as
beautiful and as strange.

After the third time the young woman
raised her bow and shot an arrow
up into the darkness.

A small,
almost colorless bird
fell to the ground at her feet.

And before anyone could pick the bird up it turned into a tall, handsome young man who took her hand.

Seeing the bird they had sought changed
into a young man, the boys fled, fearful
that they themselves might be changed into
something as unthinkable as the creatures
that inhabited their dreams.

Enormous web spinners
and giant insects.

Together the young man and beautiful woman
were about to walk out of the rain forest when
they were stopped by the notes of the old
man's flute

oorapurooo

each note perfect, mesmerizing.

oorapurooo

The young man turned on the old man,
in a rage, and the old man shot him
through the heart.

In a flash the young man disappeared and a small colorless bird flew up into the branches overhead and sang its beautiful song:

oora purooo

ooorapoorooooo

oorapooroo.

If you were to go to the rain forests of Brazil today
and were very patient and very quiet, you might hear
the beautiful song of the Uirapurú—

a song you would never, never forget.

P. K. Page, 1906 - 2010

Throughout her distinguished career, P. K. Page wrote
some of the most beautiful and haunting poems to be
found in world literature.

This adaptation of a Brazilian legend about a very special
songbird celebrates her own unique and memorable voice.

P. K. Page (1916-2010) was also an artist who painted under the name P. K. Irwin. She was the author of more than a dozen books of poetry, travel, short stories, and children's books. She won numerous prizes, including the Governor General's Prize for Poetry, received eight honorary degrees, was a Companion of the Order of Canada, a member of the Order of British Columbia and a Fellow of the Royal Society of Canada.

Kristi Bridgeman lives in Saanich, B.C. with her husband and two children. She has illustrated several books. Her fine art pieces can be found at the Art Gallery of Greater Victoria and Sooke Harbour House Gallery.

Library and Archives Canada Cataloguing in Publication

Page, P. K. (Patricia Kathleen), 1916-
        Uirapurú : based on a Brazilian legend / P.K. Page ; Kristi
Bridgeman, illustrator.

ISBN 978-0-88982-264-1

    1. Legends--Brazil. I. Bridgeman, Kristi, 1961- II. Title.

PS8531.A34U37 2010   jC813›.54   C2010-901912-1

We gratefully acknowledge the financial support of the Canada Council for the Arts, the British Columbia Arts Council through the BC Ministry of Tourism, Culture, and the Arts, and the Government of Canada through the Book Publishing Industry Development Program, for our publishing activities.

Published by
Oolichan Books
P.O. Box 2278, Fernie
British Columbia, Canada
V0B 1M0
Printed in China